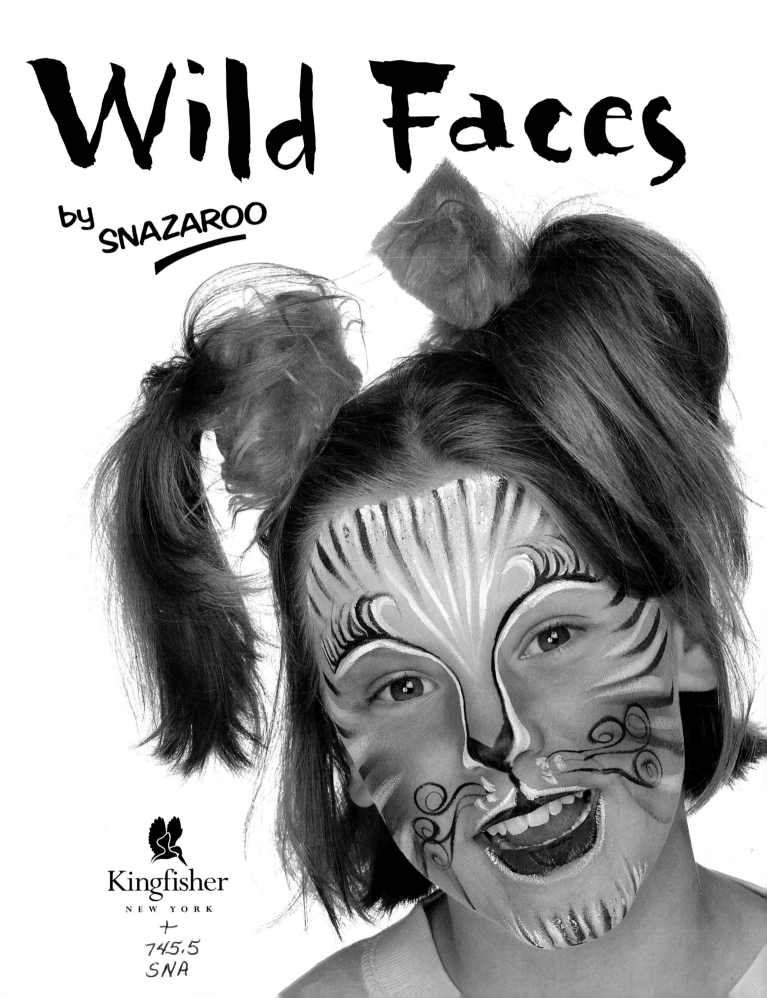

Wild Faces

by SNAZAROO

Kingfisher

NEW YORK

745.5
SNA

Contents

Introduction

Pale pink base

FACE PAINTING has become more and more popular in recent years and, with the kind of water-based face paint now available, it's possible for anyone to achieve really startling designs with just a little practice. Of all the faces we've been asked to create, animals are the most popular. In this book, therefore, we've provided plenty of animal faces for you to copy and adapt. If you're new to face painting, look at the step-by-step photos on the right, which give you the basic techniques of using face paints.

Glitter gel is a fun extra.

1 Always apply the base coat first with a sponge. Keep your sponge fairly dry. If you make it too wet, the paint may become streaky. Take the paint up to the hairline and just under the chin.

▶ *Water-based face paints come in a fantastic range of colors. Now you can also buy a pearlized paint that gives a softer sheen (see pages 27 and 31).*

Materials

The best paints to buy are water-based face paints. These are quick and easy to put on. They also dry quickly and won't smudge (as long as they don't get wet), and they're easy to wash off with a little soap and water. You can buy paints in single containers, or in palettes that contain several colors and a brush and sponge. If you're going to do a lot of face painting, it's worth buying several brushes of different thicknesses and a selection of sponges. Look for stipple sponges, which are good for creating texture.

Paint over the lips, too.

Apply brush strokes with a firm, steady hand. Try not to sketch.

Apply glitter gel with a dry brush.

2 Apply one color at a time. When painting a large patch of color—like this beak—draw the outline first with a fine brush, then fill it in with a thicker one.

3 Add paler colors before darker ones. Here, we've overlapped the colors slightly and used shorter brush strokes to give the appearance of feathers.

4 Darker colors are usually added last. Here, we've outlined the beak, painted lines on the nose and lips, and added the feathery design between the eyes—all in black.

Basics

1 Before you begin, make sure you have one or two jars of clean water handy. Remember to change the water frequently and keep all your brushes and sponges very clean.

2 Always apply water-based makeup to clean, dry skin.

3 Never use face paints on problem skin. If you're not sure, first test a small patch of paint on your model's wrist.

4 Try to keep your designs simple and quick. Young children find it hard to sit still for much more than five minutes!

5 Seat your models on a high stool or chair. Keep them steady by resting one hand on their head.

6 Always be careful when painting around the eyes. When painting the top eyelids, ask your models to keep their eyes closed until the paint has dried. Never paint too close to the bottom of the eyes.

▶ *Cats and tigers are probably the most popular animal faces of all. See pages 9 and 12–15 for inspiration.*

Pet Pals

ALL CHILDREN, especially younger ones, love having their faces painted as puppies, kittens, mice, or rabbits. These are all easy designs to start with when you are new to face painting. They're also useful for more experienced face painters working at fund-raising events or parties, with many faces to paint in a short amount of time. On very small children, keep your designs really simple. You don't even need a base coat—just paint a little nose and whiskers for a kitten and some black and white spots for a spotted dog.

Tie long hair in pigtails to look like shaggy ears.

Dizzy Dog

1 Apply a thin, light brown base over the whole face with a fairly dry sponge.

2 Using a thick brush, paint the large white patches above the eyes and in the area around the nose and lower cheeks.

3 Outline the white eye patches in chestnut brown.

4 Paint the nose and upper lip in black and outline the white area around the mouth. Then, with a fine brush, add the feathery effect at the corners of the lips, the spots, and the black lines on the cheeks and at the corners of the eyes.

5 Finally, paint the lower lip red or pink.

Take paint up to the hairline.

Patch

1 Sponge a white base all over the face, keeping the sponge fairly dry.

2 Add the black patches (being careful not to paint too close to the eye), the feathery eyebrow, the nose, and the mouth.

3 Paint on the red tongue.

A baseball cap turned sideways works well with this character.

Pink Rabbit

1 Apply a thin white base with a sponge. Using the same sponge, blend some light pink over the cheeks.

2 Paint the two pink triangular patches above the eyes with a brush.

3 Paint the area around the mouth and the teeth in white.

4 With a fine brush, add the black lines on the forehead, cheeks, and below the eyes. Outline the teeth, then add the spots above the lips and paint on the round nose.

5 Finally, paint the lips pink.

Add dots and lines on the cheeks for whiskers.

THE TWO MOUSE FACES below show how you can achieve very different effects simply by changing your base colors and adapting the features slightly. The tawny cat face looks difficult at first glance but uses only four colors. The dramatic effect is achieved by using bold overlapping brush strokes.

Naughty Mouse

1 Use a sponge to apply a thin gray base coat. Use the same sponge to blend some pink over the cheeks.

2 Paint on the white eyes and add dots over the mouth with a fine brush.

3 Add the pink nose.

4 With a brush, outline the eyes, fill in the upper lip, and add the black lines.

5 Paint the lower lip pink.

Party Mouse

1 Apply turquoise around the edges of the face with a barely damp sponge. Using the same sponge, blend pink over the cheeks and on the chin.

2 Paint the eyes and the area around the mouth pale pink.

3 Add the white teeth.

4 Add the outlines, nose, and whiskers in black.

5 Add the white highlights with a very fine brush.

Tawny Cat

1 Sponge a beige or light pink base over the whole face.

2 With a brush, paint pink above and below the eyes, down the front of the nose, and on the tip of the nose.

3 Paint tawny patches above the eyes, and brush two lines down the sides of the nose.

4 Paint on the white muzzle, then do all the black outlines with a fine brush. Add lines around the eyes and down the nose.

5 With a wide, flat brush, add the white, black, and brown dashes, one color at a time, to create the appearance of fur.

Brush on the paint in the direction that the fur would grow. _____

Add a touch of glitter above the eyes and around the nose.

Black cardboard ears attached to an elastic headband.

Barnyard Buddies

SIMPLY PAINTING a whole animal on a cheek, hand, or arm is quick and fun to do. Look for other barnyard animal motifs you could copy, such as a munching cow or a mother hen with her yellow chicks. For a dramatic full face, try painting this white feathery duck.

Fluffy Duck

1 Using a sponge, apply a white base over the whole face.

2 Paint the blue patches above the eyes with a brush.

3 Paint on the wide yellow beak.

4 Add the black lines around the eyes, nostrils, and beak.

5 Paint the lower lip dark blue, extending the natural line of the mouth.

6 Finish with the feather design. Paint the pale blue V-shapes first, then add the orange, then the dark blue.

Rooster

Paint in the red and green base colors, add white and yellow highlights, then outline in black. Add the bird's red crest and brown feet with a fine brush, and put a dot in its eye.

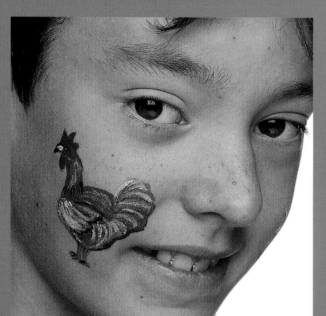

Pink Pig

As with the lamb, add the base color first—here a pale pink. Add darker pink under the pig's belly, then outline in brown. Finish with some tufts of green grass around its feet.

Leaping Lamb

Paint the woolly white coat, add the black legs, tail, and head, then paint black swirls over the coat with a fine brush.

10

A white feather
boa makes a
perfect headdress.

Always keep
paint away
from the eyes.

Wildcat

1 Sponge beige paint over the center of the face.

2 Using the same sponge, add white over the nose and mouth, and then chestnut or rust-colored paint over the rest of the face.

3 With a thick brush, paint the dark brown lines over the eyes. Then, with a finer brush, add the two lines down the sides of the nose.

4 Paint the cat's top teeth on the model's lower lip and the bottom teeth on the chin.

5 Paint the rest of the mouth shape in black, then add the black nose and spots.

6 Add red around the eyes and paint the whiskers.

Colorful cats

C **ATS CAN BE REALISTIC**, like our fierce wildcat, or much more fanciful, like the fantasy cats below. Even though they look very different, each of these cats has a dark nose, boldly painted whiskers, and distinctive curved lines or patches over the eyes. We've given a mottled texture to the wildcat by applying yellow paint with a stipple sponge. On the fantasy cats, we've used a touch of glitter.

Pink Cat

There are no rules about which base colors to use on a fantasy cat, but choose different color combinations carefully. Here, the bright pink and purple work well together, especially with white.

Sponge paint into the hair.

Add silver glitter with a fine brush.

Add gold glitter on the forehead and chin for extra sparkle.

Paint curly whiskers and eyebrows with a fine brush.

Curved lines should be painted in one bold, continuous brush stroke.

Blue Cat

To paint this cat, first apply a blue base, then sponge yellow over the forehead, down the sides of the face, and over the chin. Paint the dark blue lines first, then add the white highlights. The lines around the outside of the face have been painted from the outside toward the middle of the face, and the colors have been blended slightly, to soften.

13

Big Cats

LIONS AND TIGERS have the same basic features as cats and kittens. Here, you can see that each face has a similar nose, with a short black line running from just under the nose to the upper lip. The faces also have white muzzles and fan-shaped patches above the eyes. Coloring varies—the lion has a golden-yellow base, and the tigers have distinctive orange and black markings. Fur patterns have been achieved in different ways—with fine, feathery brush strokes, bold lines, or with a stippling effect.

Hands

Hands (and feet) can easily be painted to match your animal faces. Here, we've painted a striped tiger hand in orange and black.

Golden Lion

1 Apply a yellow base over the whole face with a barely damp sponge. Then, with a clean sponge, dab white over the area around the mouth.

2 Using a brush, paint the dark brown lines over the eyebrows. Then add the two finer lines curving from the eyes, out over the cheeks, and back to the corners of the mouth.

3 Paint white above the eyes and add the whiskers.

4 Paint the lower lip red, then add the black nose and spots.

5 Finish with the feathery lines around the face, adding a little gold glitter for extra texture.

Keep your hand steady when you brush on the two brown lines.

Use the side of a wide, flat brush to give the texture of short, spiky fur.

Sponge paint into the hair or make a set of ears out of fake fur.

Saber-Toothed Tiger

1 Sponge a yellow base over the whole face with a fairly dry sponge. Use the same sponge to blend orange paint around the outer edges of the face and white above the eyebrows.

2 Paint the muzzle and the sharp fangs in white.

3 Add the black nose, fill in the upper lip, and paint the fine, feathery outline around the muzzle and teeth.

4 Paint the black fur using the side of a brush. Start with the area between the eyes, then do the cheeks. Use the same technique to apply white paint between the black brush strokes.

5 Add a touch of yellow over the eyes.

6 Finish with the red lines under the eyes and the drops of red on the teeth for blood.

Brush on stripes from the outside of the face toward the center.

Little Tiger

1 Apply a base coat as close to the model's own natural coloring as possible.

2 Using a stipple sponge, dab some red paint over the cheeks and forehead.

3 Paint the rust fan-shaped lines over the eyebrows.

4 Add the white lines above the eyes and around the mouth.

5 Paint in the black nose, mouth, and whiskers.

6 Add the lines under the eyes and the bold black and brown stripes around the face.

15

Spots and Stripes

Giraffe

1 Sponge on a yellow base coat, then paint the beige patch around the mouth.

2 Paint the brown eyes and nostrils and outline the mouth.

3 Add the black lines over the lips, extending the lines over each cheek.

4 Paint the yellow, squarish patches, then outline in brown.

SOME ANIMALS have such distinctive markings on their coats that it is easy to make them into effective face-painting designs. Spotted leopards, striped tigers and zebras, and giraffes with their yellow and brown patches, are especially easy to adapt. Spots and stripes also make good body-painting designs, as shown in the photograph below.

Paint in whole blocks of yellow before outlining in brown.

Body Painting

Body painting can be extremely dramatic. If you're doing it for a stage production, use bold patterns that will show up from a distance. Don't forget to cover every part of the body that will show, including underneath the arms, hands, and feet.

Snow Leopard

1 Apply a white base coat over the whole face with a fairly dry sponge.

2 Paint the white eye patches and the area around the mouth with a large brush.

3 Paint black over the eyelids and add the black outlines, nose, and whiskers.

4 Using your finger, dab pink and black spots over the face, slightly overlapping each one. Add touches of silver glitter over the spots with a dry brush.

5 Finish by painting the lower lip pink.

Keep the whiskers very fine and slightly curved.

Zebra

1 Apply a white base. Then, with the same sponge, dab a little pink over the cheeks, forehead, and chin.

2 Paint the black circles around the eyes (keeping the paint away from the area right under the eyes), then the nose and mouth.

3 Brush on the black stripes.

17

Bear Hugs

Panda

To paint this panda, sponge on a white base, then paint the black design. The eye patches are round at the top but slope down over the cheeks to make the bear look a little sad and in need of a hug.

BEAR FACES can be easy and quick to do just by sponging on a plain base coat, then adding one or two extra colors with a thick brush—like the panda and teddy bears shown here—or they can take longer, like the brown bear with its painted fur. Paint a bear's nose and mouth the same way as you would a cat's, but without the whiskers. The main difference between a bear's and a cat's face is the eyes—for a bear, keep the patches around the eyes round rather than making them pointed or fan-shaped.

Teddy Bears

1 Paint a light brown base over the whole face using a slightly damp sponge.

2 Paint large white circles around the eyes with a thick brush. Make the circles slightly thicker at the top.

3 With a brush, paint the eyebrows, mouth, nose, and dots black.

▶ *These teddy bear faces are ideal for small children who find it hard to sit still for long.*

Brown Bear

1 Using a sponge and a little water, apply a light brown base over the whole face.

2 Paint the round brown eye patches with a brush.

3 Using a fine brush, paint the black nose and mouth. Add a thin line of black right under the upper lip, and extend the line of the mouth.

4 Again with a fine brush, add several shades of brown all over the face. Use light, feathery strokes to give the impression of fur.

Add dots over the muzzle with the point of a fine brush.

Curve the line of the mouth upward.

Monkey Business

White-Faced Monkey

1 Keeping your sponge fairly dry, apply a light brown or beige base over the whole face.

2 Paint the large white patch over the center of the face.

3 Paint dark brown around the eyes.

4 Apply a little light brown above and below the mouth, using a sponge or brush.

5 Paint the black nostrils and mouth. Add the fine lines around the mouth. Then, with a thick brush, add the black and white stripes.

IT'S AMAZING how easy it is to change the shape and appearance of someone's face with makeup. The eyes on these two faces look small and deep-set because they have been outlined in dark colors. The baboon face looks long and pointed because we have lengthened the nose and taken the paint over the lips, using a bright color to make it stand out. Both these faces will take practice, and you'll need an older model who will sit still for you.

Don't paint too close to the eyes.

Baboon

1 Paint the nose and the heart-shaped area around the mouth bright red.

2 Paint black over the eyes, and outline the sides of the red nose.

3 Paint the dark blue area with a brush.

4 Paint dark brown above and below the eyes and on the cheeks.

5 Using a finer brush, paint lots of small, feathery strokes over the rest of the face in dark brown, medium brown, and light brown.

6 Again with a fine brush, highlight the forehead in white and add the white highlights over the blue paint.

7 Paint black over and around the mouth, then add the feathery white highlights over the top.

Brush paint into the hair. Don't forget to paint the ears, too.

Red Parrot

1 Apply a thin, peach-colored base over the whole face.

2 Paint the green ovals around the eyes, then outline them in red.

3 Paint the red beak.

4 Outline the beak in black, then paint the black patch over the red beak.

5 Paint the red and blue feathers.

Use a fine brush to create the feathery design.

Lift the brush toward the end of each stroke for a softer look.

The black part of the beak should be narrower than the mouth.

Birds of Paradise

Peacock

First paint the peacock's pale blue body shape between the eyes and over the nose. Add the dark blue wings and crest, then paint the white and black "eyes" on the feathers. Add the yellow beak, outline it in black, paint the lips blue, and finish with a little glitter.

BIRDS MAKE GOOD FACE-PAINTING DESIGNS. From cute little parakeets to exotic tropical parrots . . . let your imagination soar! Again, you can make your designs simple to suit a younger child—just paint a wide yellow or red beak over the nose and mouth and brush some brightly colored feathers around the edges of the face. The peacock mask is especially good for older children and is a popular party face. Other birds can easily be painted as masks in the same way (see the butterfly masks on the next page).

Pink bird

1 Paint in the wide beak with a brush, outlining the shape in yellow first, then filling it in with the same color.

2 Paint the black mouth, the laughter lines, and the lines by the nostrils and over the nose.

3 With a brush, paint bright pink, purple, and white feathers over the forehead and on the chin.

▶ *Feather boas make perfect headdresses for tropical birds. Tie them in place under the chin or at the nape of the neck.*

23

Creepy Crawlies

Honeycomb

1 Apply a yellow base over the whole face with a sponge.

2 Paint the orange hexagons across the forehead and down the cheeks, then outline them in black.

3 Paint the yellow bodies of the bee and fly, then their white wings.

4 Outline the wings in black, paint the heads, then add the bee's stripes.

5 With a fine brush, add the black detail on the wings, then highlight the honeycomb with a touch of white paint.

CREEPY CRAWLIES are always popular with children. If they have wings, they work well as a painted mask across the eyes. Otherwise, you can paint the whole creature as a small motif on the cheek. It's also fun to paint an insect crawling up your model's arm or leg. Remember that the smaller the motif, the fewer colors you should use so that the picture stands out clearly. If you paint a butterfly mask in bright, bold colors, you probably will not need to apply a base coat. Remember to make the pattern on your butterfly's wings symmetrical.

Always paint blocks of solid color before outlining in black.

Bumblebee

A bee can be painted as a black mask over the eyes, with a bright yellow base. You could also paint a simple bee face by brushing yellow and black stripes horizontally across the face.

Use a thin brush to paint the fine black veins.

Blue Butterfly

Paint the butterfly's pink body first, then paint the pale blue, pale green, orange, and turquoise shapes above the eyes and over the cheeks. Paint the black outline, then the white antennae and the lines on the body.

Paint a large black spot on each lower wing.

Pink Butterfly

1 Apply a thin yellow base over the face with a fairly dry sponge.

2 Paint the deep pink above the eyes first. Then, working from the top down, paint each band of color with a brush.

3 Outline each section in black with a fine brush, then add the black dots.

4 Add the antennae and the detail down the nose.

5 Decorate with glitter gel, applying each color of glitter with a clean, dry brush.

6 Paint the lips deep blue and white.

Gold mesh makes
a perfect party
headdress. Wrap it
around the head
like a turban.

Party Motifs

Scorpion

1 Paint the shape of the scorpion on the cheek in orange, then fill in with the same color.

2 With a fine brush, outline the scorpion in black.

3 With the same brush, add the black detail on each section of the scorpion's body.

4 Add white highlights and paint the eyes.

5 Outline the eyes with a fine brush and add dots for the pupils.

SPIDERS AND SCORPIONS are popular motifs with teenagers—especially at Halloween. Webs take a little practice. Find a good photograph to work from and keep the lines as fine and delicate as you can.

Curve the lines on the web inward.

Paint two thin black lines right under the eyes to make them stand out.

Spider

1 Sponge on a pale yellow base. Then, with the same sponge, add a little white over the forehead and down the nose. Here, we've used pearlized water-based makeup to give the skin a soft sheen.

2 Paint the spider web in black, using a fine brush.

3 Paint the spider. Use one or two colors—here, black white, and a touch of red.

4 Complete the effect with bright red lips and a little silver glitter to highlight the web.

Something Fishy

TROPICAL FISH and other sea creatures are wonderful for face painting because of their bright, exotic colors and patterns. Look at books to get more ideas—jellyfish, sharks, beautiful shells, and angelfish would all make fantastic face-painting designs. Here are some tiger fish and leaping dolphins to get you started. Omit a base coat, or sponge blue water-based makeup over the whole face or just one cheek, as shown below.

Tiger Fish

1 Paint the fish shapes in orange with a brush then fill in with the same color.

2 Outline both fish in black, then add their black stripes and eyes.

3 Paint on the white stripes with the edge of a wide brush (see more on this technique on page 15).

4 Paint the white bubbles with the tip of a brush.

5 Paint the seaweed in green and white.

Flamingo and Crab

Sponge some pale blue over part of each face. Mark out your shapes first in pink or orange, then fill them in with the same color. Again, we've added touches of glitter gel to the designs for a party look.

Brush a little white over the dolphins' backs and tails, to highlight.

Use the edge of a wide brush to achieve this effect.

Dolphins

Dolphins are fairly easy to paint, but you may need to practice on paper first to get their shape right. If you want to give the dolphins' skin a shiny texture, use blue pearlized water-based makeup. Outline the dolphins in a darker blue to make them stand out, and add some white bubbles.

Going Green

Green Frog

1 Sponge a thin yellow base over the whole face.

2 Paint around the outside of the face in green with a thick brush. Use a darker green to paint the chin.

3 Paint the white areas above the eyes, then outline them in brown.

4 Paint the lips brown, extending the lines on either side to make a wide frog's mouth.

5 Paint dark blue lines over the forehead and on either side of the mouth.

GREEN SCALY OR SLIMY CREATURES are always popular faces. The special pearlized makeup we used for the spider on page 27 and the dolphins on page 29 works especially well if you want to paint shiny reptile skin. We've used it for the dinosaur face on the right, but have painted the green frog in ordinary water-based face paint.

Sponge a little green paint into your model's hair. It will wash out easily with ordinary shampoo.

It's fun to paint the ears and body, too.

Terrible Lizard

1 Apply a pearlized light green base with a damp sponge.

2 Using the same sponge, apply a darker shade of pearlized green around the outer edges of the face. Again with the same sponge, blend a little red over the cheeks and right under the eyes.

3 With a brush, paint the shapes above the eyes and over the nose. Use a large brush to blend the green paint inward. You will need to do this before the green outline dries, so work quickly and apply the paint a little at a time.

4 Paint the green mouth, just over the model's chin.

5 Paint the lips white, add the white teeth, then outline the teeth in black with a fine brush.

6 Paint the black nostrils over your model's upper lip.

Gallery

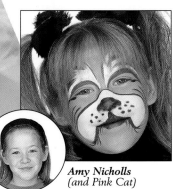

Amy Nicholls
(and Pink Cat)

Bryony Holiman

THE PUBLISHERS would like to thank all the models— who look very different without their makeup—and face painters Lauren Staton and Wilhelmina Barnden.

Many thanks also to George Jackson (Patch and Leaping Lamb), Victoria Sloman (Party Mouse and Crab), Eleanor Yeandle (Pink Rabbit), Louise Ahearn (Cheeky Mouse), Charles Bullock (Frog and Panda), Josephine Aldridge (Baboon, Blue Cat and Spider), and Kelly Randall (Zebra).

Lisa Herbert
(and Scorpion)

Katy Nicholls

Emma Ryan
(and Brown Bear and Terrible Lizard)

James Bullock

Kate Gibbs

Amy Wigglesworth

Andrea Stradling

Luke Ngakane

Gemma Jeffs

Jonathan Aldridge
(and Cockerel, Sheep and Honeycomb)

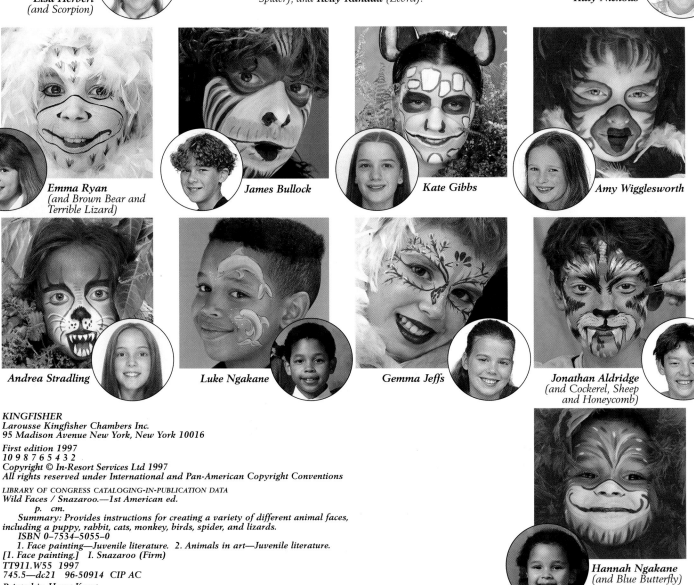

Hannah Ngakane
(and Blue Butterfly)

KINGFISHER
Larousse Kingfisher Chambers Inc.
95 Madison Avenue New York, New York 10016

First edition 1997
10 9 8 7 6 5 4 3 2
Copyright © In-Resort Services Ltd 1997
All rights reserved under International and Pan-American Copyright Conventions

LIBRARY OF CONGRESS CATALOGING-IN-PUBLICATION DATA
Wild Faces / Snazaroo.—1st American ed.
        p.   cm.
    Summary: Provides instructions for creating a variety of different animal faces, including a puppy, rabbit, cats, monkey, birds, spider, and lizards.
    ISBN 0–7534–5055–0
    1. Face painting—Juvenile literature. 2. Animals in art—Juvenile literature.
[1. Face painting.]   I. Snazaroo (Firm)
TT911.W55 1997
745.5—dc21   96-50914 CIP AC
Printed in Hong Kong